Alone in the Night

Other titles by Holly Webb

Alone in the Night

Holly Webb

Illustrated by Sophy Williams

LITTLE TIGER

LONDON

For Tom

STRIPES PUBLISHING LIMITED
An imprint of Little Tiger Group
1 Coda Studios, 189 Munster Road, London SW6 6AW

Imported into the EEA by Penguin Random House Ireland,
Morrison Chambers, 32 Nassau Street, Dublin D02 YH68

A paperback original
First published in Great Britain in 2009

Text copyright © Holly Webb, 2009
Illustrations copyright © Sophy Williams, 2009
Author photograph copyright © Charlotte Knee Photography

ISBN: 978-1-84715-094-3

A CIP catalogue record for this book is available from the British Library.

Printed and bound in the UK.

The Forest Stewardship Council® (FSC®) is a global, not-for-profit
organization dedicated to the promotion of responsible forest management
worldwide. FSC defines standards based on agreed principles for
responsible forest stewardship that are supported by environmental, social,
and economic stakeholders. To learn more, visit www.fsc.org

10 9

Chapter One

"Jasmine! Hurry up! You're going to be late for school!" Jasmine's mum glanced at her watch – and then at all the other children wearing the same uniform as her daughter, who were streaming past the end of their road.

Jasmine looked up. "Oh, but, I was just saying hello to Tiger, Mum!" The marmalade tabby cat sitting on the wall ducked his head so Jasmine could rub his ears. Then he stood up and leaned over to bump the side of his head against her chin. Jasmine had read lots of books about cats and knew that he wasn't just being cute. He was rubbing his scent glands on her. It was pretty cute, too, though. All the cats in the street loved Jasmine – which is why it always took her so long to get to school.

"Jasmine, we left the house ten minutes ago and we haven't even got past next door!" Her mum sighed. "You're going to be *late*."

"Sorry, Mum." Jasmine smiled at her apologetically. "Let's run!"

She was just picking up her school bag when she stopped again. "Oh, Mum, look! In next door's window!"

She pointed across the garden.

"Oh, a kitten."

"Mum! A *gorgeous* kitten! I haven't seen her before. Did you know the new people next door had a kitten?"

The kitten was tiny, perched right in the middle of the big window sill, which made her look tinier still. Jasmine could just about make out her beautiful stripy brown tabby markings.

"No, I didn't," Mum said, leading her away. Jasmine walked backwards, still staring at the kitten, who stared back. "You know we haven't really said any more than a quick hello while they were unpacking."

"Poor little kitten. They must have left her all alone while they've gone to work," Jasmine said sadly.

"Oh, Jasmine! Cats don't mind being on their own," her mum laughed. "Besides, how do you even know that kitten's a she? It could be a boy."

"She just looked like a she," Jasmine said. "And cats do get lonely, Mum, especially when they're only babies."

"I'm sure they'll play with her when they get home," Mum comforted her. "Now run!"

Jasmine turned out to be right – the kitten was a girl. Her mum invited Helen, the new lady next door, round for coffee, and found out all about her beautiful cat.

"She's called Star," Jasmine told her best friend Lara, as they walked home from school together. "She's got such cute tabby stripes; she's really gorgeous." Jasmine sighed. "She looks exactly my dream cat – you know, the one I'd really like to have for my own some day."

"Oh, you're so lucky having her next door. She might come into your garden," Lara said enviously. "Do you know how old she is?"

"Nearly three months. They were given her by a friend whose cat had kittens. They were a bit worried she'd be upset by the move, but she doesn't mind. Except she's desperate to go out!"

"Can't they let her out?" Lara asked.

"Not until she's had all her vaccinations in a couple of weeks' time," Jasmine explained. "See you tomorrow!" she called, as they got to her gate.

Over the next few weeks, Jasmine watched for Star every time she walked past the house next door and always waved hello. Sometimes, if she was sitting on the window sill, the little cat would stand up on her back legs and scrabble hopefully at the glass with her paws, as though she hoped she might be able to slip through and come out for Jasmine to stroke her. Jasmine wished she could, too.

Star finished her wash and looked thoughtfully round the garden. She still wasn't very used to being outside. In fact, today was the first day that her owners had left her in the house with the cat flap unlocked. She'd been allowed out all on her own a few times over the weekend, and they'd put out big bowls of cat crunchies to make sure she came back. Of course she had! She loved her house, and her basket, and her food bowls, and her people. Exploring was fun too, that was all.

She headed to the end of the garden. The brambles there were fascinating, full of nests and tunnels and hidey-holes. When she'd finally finished investigating and wriggled out again, her eyes were sparkling with excitement. She licked the fur round her mouth thoughtfully, trying to get rid of the rather strange taste of beetle. Beetles looked delicious, like walking cat crunchies, but they didn't taste good.

Star sat down in the middle of the lawn, closing her eyes for a moment and feeling the warm autumn sunshine on her fur. Then she went and rolled around in a pile of dried leaves. When she'd got bored of that game, she stretched out her front paws and then her back paws, and looked for something to do next. There was a snail moving very slowly along a leaf just next to her, and she watched that for a little while, but she'd learned from the beetle, and didn't try to eat it.

That was when she spotted the gap under the fence. Star didn't really know what the fence was. She didn't quite understand that there was a whole new garden on the other side of it. But she knew that the little hole looked interesting.

The gap wasn't very big, and she had to scratch a little at the earth underneath to get through. Star still had little soft indoor kitten paws, with apricot-pink pads, and digging her way under the fence rubbed off a little of their newness. It felt good.

She emerged in next door's garden and gave herself a quick wash. Then she looked round with interest.

Suddenly she caught sight of Jasmine. Her eyes widened – as Jasmine was so quiet she'd thought she was alone. But she didn't dive back under the fence. Star recognized the girl – she was the friendly one who always waved when she walked past the house.

It was the middle of the half-term holiday. Jasmine was in the garden putting the leftover toast crusts from breakfast out on the bird table when she caught a little greyish-brown flash in the corner of her eye. She turned her head slowly, hoping to see what sort of bird it was. But it wasn't a sparrow hopping about in the bushes. It was a cat.

Not just any cat... *The* cat. It was little Star, from next door.

She was squeezing herself under the fence, wriggling and scrabbling, with such a determined expression on her face that Jasmine had to bite her lip to stop herself from giggling – she didn't want to scare Star away.

The kitten finally popped out from under the fence like she'd been pushed and twitched her tail crossly. Then she sat down to have a wash, brushing her paw thoroughly round her ears in case she'd got them grubby fighting her way through.

Jasmine perched on the garden bench and watched her, not even wanting to breathe too deeply in case she frightened the tiny creature. She'd been hoping to meet Star properly for so long, and the kitten was only a few metres away.

Now Star had obviously seen her. She stood up daintily and padded over to Jasmine. No one had stroked her since Helen and Andy left for work, and even though exploring was fun, she wanted someone to fuss over her. She stopped a little way away, just far enough to make a run for it if Jasmine turned out not to be friendly, and gave a hopeful little mew.

Jasmine reached out her hand slowly. She couldn't believe Star had come this close – she'd thought that such a little kitten would be too nervous. She could almost touch Star's nose, but she didn't. She just held her fingers out, and whispered, "Here, puss, hello, Star…"

Star's ears pricked slightly. The girl knew her name! That had to be good.

She pranced a few steps closer and rubbed her head affectionately against Jasmine's leg.

Jasmine laughed and stroked Star's ears, and Star made a big leap and sprang on to the bench next to her, then climbed into Jasmine's lap. There she gave a contented little sigh and closed her eyes, massaging Jasmine's jeans with her little needle-sharp claws. Good. Proper stroking.

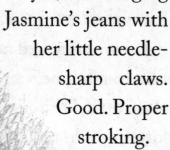

Jasmine smiled down at her, wishing she had a beautiful kitten of her very own. It was such a pity her mum and dad weren't really pet people. But maybe gorgeous little Star could help convince them?

From then on, Jasmine always looked out for Star in the garden, and Star soon worked out what time Jasmine got home from school. If she was bored, or wanted someone to play with, she would wriggle under the fence – she'd had to make the hole quite a lot bigger by now – and jump from the bench on to the kitchen window sill. Then she would mew plaintively for Jasmine to come out and see her.

Jasmine's mum thought it was funny at first, but then she got a bit worried. What if the next-door neighbours minded about Jasmine spending all this time fussing over their kitten?

One day the kitchen window was open – Jasmine's mum had been cooking chilli for dinner and wanted to let the smell out – and when Jasmine came into the kitchen she saw Star nosing curiously around the gap, obviously wondering if she was allowed to step in through the window.

Jasmine didn't even think. She just held out her hand and made puss-puss noises to Star, tempting her in. She couldn't imagine anything nicer than cuddling Star in her own kitchen. Unless it was in her bedroom, of course…

Jasmine's mum was horrified when she came up to see how Jasmine was getting on with her homework. "Jasmine! What's that cat doing in here?" she cried.

Star gave a nervous little squeak and disappeared off Jasmine's lap under the desk.

Jasmine glared at her mum and crouched down to try and coax her out. "You frightened her!"

"She frightened me!" her mum retorted. "She's not meant to be in our house, Jasmine, she's next door's cat!"

"I bet they wouldn't mind," Jasmine muttered. She knew she shouldn't really have let Star in, but she'd been so lonely, mewing on the window sill. "They don't get home till later, Mum; she just wanted a cuddle!"

"Jasmine, she's not ours. She'll end up getting confused about where she lives – she's only little. Put her out!" her mum said firmly. And Jasmine had to gather Star up and take her back downstairs.

"Sorry, Star!" Jasmine murmured, as she slipped the kitten out of the back door. Her mum was watching, her arms folded sternly, and Jasmine knew she'd be pushing her luck if she went outside too. But it was getting dark and had started to rain. She felt so guilty putting Star out in the cold and wet.

Star watched the door close, looking up at it sadly. Why hadn't Jasmine's mother wanted her? She didn't understand. She shook her whiskers, feeling confused, then slunk across the garden, under the fence and back through her cat flap.

Chapter Two

After Mum had made her take Star outside, Jasmine didn't risk letting her in the house again, however much she wanted to. For the next few weeks she played with Star in the garden instead, even though it was November and freezing cold. Star's lovely furry coat kept her a lot warmer than Jasmine's blue school anorak, but she didn't want to miss out on playing with the kitten.

"Jasmine! Come on in, it's tea time!" Jasmine's mum called from the back door.

Jasmine picked up Star and put her gently on top of the fence – she liked jumping on to it now she was a bit bigger, instead of scrabbling underneath. "Bye, Star! See you tomorrow," she murmured, stroking the little cat's nose. Star was in that funny stage now where she was half-kitten, half-cat and all legs.

Her mum was still looking out of the back door. "Aren't you frozen? Look, your hands are bright red; where are your gloves?"

Jasmine wiggled her fingers, which were feeling quite numb now. "I was stroking Star; you can't stroke a cat with gloves on, Mum."

Her mum shook her head, smiling. "You and that cat."

Star jumped lightly down from the wall and trotted back to her cat flap. She was very cold and she wanted to go inside. But when she nudged her cat flap with her nose, it didn't open. Star butted it harder, but she only hurt her nose. She mewed crossly. Then she tried scratching at the cat flap, but that didn't work either. The flap was stuck, and it wouldn't budge.

Star mewed again, louder this time, hoping her owners would hear. But no one came. Miserably, she crept away and hid under a bush close to the door, waiting for the house lights to go on to show her owners were home.

It seemed as though she waited for ages, while the garden grew darker and darker, and ever more cold. Even her tail ached with it. It was too cold to sleep, and she was so hungry. She got up and went to stare sadly through the cat flap at her food bowl. Usually her owners would be home by now, she was sure. Where were they? Star didn't like being on her own. She liked people, and being stroked and petted. She looked back across the dark garden to Jasmine's house. If only she could go inside. It would be so lovely and warm in there.

Suddenly the fur on her back rose up as she sensed that another cat was in her garden, and not one she liked. She'd met quite a few other cats over the last few weeks. Some had been friendly, and some had warned her away. She jumped round, whiskers bristling, and saw an enormous dark shape creeping towards her. A dark shape that *hissed*.

Star squeaked with fright and backed up against the wall, darting a quick, desperate glance at her cat flap. But it was still shut tight.

The black cat padded closer and hissed again, and then swiped at her with one huge dark paw, sending her skidding away.

Star skittered across the garden and dived for the hole under the fence. Frantically, she squeezed her way through, even though it was really far too tight, and shot out into Jasmine's garden. At least the hole was too small for that huge black cat to follow her. Star ran over to Jasmine's back door and let out a panicky howl, hoping Jasmine would come and rescue her.

She'd been right. The hole was too small for the black cat. But she could hear him scrambling up the fence…

Jasmine was asleep, dreaming of a horrible spelling test, when her teacher suddenly turned into a mewing cat. She wriggled and turned over, muttering in her sleep. But the meowing didn't stop, and eventually she woke up, blinking worriedly into the darkness. That was Star!

Jasmine hopped out of bed and dragged on her dressing gown. She was leaning over the top of the stairs when her dad came out of the living room.

"Oh, did they wake you, Jasmine?

Don't be scared; it's just some cats fighting in the garden. I'm going to chase them away."

Jasmine shook her head anxiously, and ran down the stairs towards him. "No, Dad, don't! That sounds like Star, the kitten from next door. I'm sure she's not fighting. She's really scared, I can tell."

Her dad sighed. "Your mum said you'd fallen in love with that cat. Come on, then, let's see what's going on."

He opened the back door, and there on the step, shivering, was a tiny little tabby thing, her fur all up on end and her tail looking like a feather duster. Lurking a couple of metres away, its eyes shining green in the light from the kitchen, was the biggest black cat

Jasmine had ever seen.

"Oh! It's Sam, from down the road. He's always fighting. He's only got half an ear, and Mrs James has to take him to the vet about once a fortnight. We can't let him fight with Star, he's so huge he'd just squash her!" Jasmine went out on to the step, not caring about her bare feet. "Shoo, Sam! Go home, bad cat!"

Sam backed off, but only a little way. Star gave a miserable little mew, and Jasmine picked her up gently. "Dad, please can we bring her inside? I know the Murrays wouldn't mind, not if she was going to get hurt."

Her dad sighed and looked over at her mum, who'd come into the kitchen to see what was happening.

"Why can't she go home?" Mum asked, sounding reluctant. "Hasn't she got a cat flap?"

Jasmine shrugged. "Maybe she's too scared to get past Sam?"

"I'll nip next door and see if the

Murrays are home. It didn't look like their lights were on though." Dad went round to the front of the house.

Jasmine cuddled Star, feeling her heart racing inside her fragile body. She was still such a little cat.

Dad came back, shaking his head. "No, they're definitely out."

Jasmine's mum sighed. "Well, maybe we had better hold on to her. Just till Helen and Andy get home. They must have gone out for the evening."

Even though it was late, Jasmine's mum and dad let her stay downstairs with Star – it was a Friday evening, so there was no school the next day. And when Jasmine pointed out that Star probably hadn't had any tea, Mum even found a tin of tuna for her.

But it got later and later, and Jasmine couldn't stop yawning. Star was curled up fast asleep on her lap on the sofa, and Jasmine's mum shook her head, laughing.

"Go up to bed, Jasmine. And yes, you can take her with you, otherwise I should think she'll howl herself silly in the kitchen. We'll just have to take her back in the morning."

Jasmine looked up at her in delight. "Really?" She had been trying so hard not to yawn in case Mum sent her off to bed, but she'd never thought they'd let her take Star upstairs, not after what Mum had said last time.

She stood up, draping sleepy little Star over her shoulder like a soft, furry scarf, and crept upstairs. She set Star down on her bed while she took off her dressing gown, then snuggled carefully under the duvet, trying not to disturb her.

Jasmine was just drifting off to sleep when she heard a quiet purring, just next to her ear, as Star burrowed down beside her. Jasmine smiled in her sleep and felt like purring, too.

The next morning Jasmine slept late after her exciting night, and it was nine o'clock when she and Star wandered downstairs. It had been so lovely waking up and finding a cat curled up next to her!

Star sat on Jasmine's lap and sniffed hopefully at the toast. Jasmine smiled. "I think Star's hungry, Mum!"

Jasmine's mum looked at her worriedly. "I wonder what she usually has for breakfast? I don't want to make her sick with too much tuna."

Jasmine's dad looked over at them. "We ought to let the Murrays know where she is – they'll be worrying about her."

Jasmine sighed. She was enjoying pretending Star was hers, but it looked like the game wouldn't last long.

She was just finishing her toast when the doorbell rang, and her mum went to answer it. Jasmine could hear Mum chatting to someone, and then she came back in with Helen and Andy from next door.

Star gave a delighted little *prrp*, and jumped off Jasmine's lap, scampering over to Helen.

"That's not very grateful!" Helen laughed. "Jasmine, your mum says you saved Star from that great big black cat from down the road. Thank you for rescuing her." She shook her head. "She's been wandering off at night quite a bit recently. I know she's just getting bigger and braver, but I wish she wouldn't. Oh well. Maybe she'll be a bit less daring for a while after her scare."

Star trotted back over and rubbed her head up against Jasmine's dressing gown. She was delighted to see her owners, but she did love Jasmine, too.

Helen gave Jasmine a thoughtful look, watching the way Star was snuggling against her.

While Jasmine said goodbye to Star, the Murrays went to talk to her mum and dad in the hallway.

"Jasmine, do you think you could do us a huge favour?" said Helen, as she came back into the kitchen and gathered up Star. "We're going away for three weeks over Christmas, and we haven't quite decided what to do with this little one. Star's such a friendly thing, we think she'd hate a cattery, where no one had much time to play with her." She paused. "Would you like to look after her for us?"

Jasmine's eyes opened wide with delight and she looked hopefully at her mum and dad. To take care of Star, for three whole weeks! She couldn't imagine anything she'd like more.

Chapter Three

Jasmine was counting down the days until the Murrays went away. She and her mum went round next door after school one night, so that the Murrays could go through everything Jasmine would need to know. They weren't going on holiday for another few days, but they wanted to get things organized in advance.

Star met them at the door, mewing with delight at the sight of Jasmine.

Helen laughed. "This was such a good idea! I was really worried about Star being miserable at a cattery. Come in."

They sat down at the kitchen table to look at a list that Helen had made of all the things she thought Jasmine would need to know, like the phone number of their vet, just in case.

Mum frowned. "I hope you can manage all this, Jasmine," she said, looking at the part about measuring out Star's special food so she didn't have too much.

"Don't worry, Mum, of course I can," Jasmine told her. "And I'll get up earlier so I can pop in on Star before school to feed her."

But when they got home, Jasmine couldn't help worrying a little, too. Not about feeding Star and looking after her properly, she was sure she could do that. No, she was worried about all the time Star would be on her own in the Murrays' house. She was a cat who loved attention and fuss – that's why she came into Jasmine's garden all the time. How would she feel about being alone every night? Now that it was nearly December, it was getting really cold. Mum wasn't going to let Jasmine sit out in the garden with Star for ages if it started snowing!

Maybe Mum would let me bring her inside for some of the time? Jasmine wondered to herself. *I'm sure Helen and Andy wouldn't mind... Oh!*

Jasmine smiled excitedly. She had just had the most brilliant idea.

What if she looked after Star at her house, instead? It would be like having a cat of her very own!

Now all she had to do was persuade Mum and Dad...

"But we don't want a cat in the house, Jasmine," Mum said. "It's all arranged, you'll feed Star next door."

Jasmine nodded. "I know, but it would be so much better if she was here. She's so friendly, Mum, she'd hate being on her own all day. And she'd be company for you while you're working." She looked at her mum hopefully. It wasn't just that she really wanted to have Star to stay – she was sure that Mum and Dad would fall in love with Star if they saw more of her. And if Jasmine could look after Star fabulously and give her back to the Murrays as the world's best-cared-for cat, wouldn't her parents be tempted to let her have a cat of her own? Once they knew how lovely it would be to have a cat in the house?

"Pets are a bit messy, Jasmine," Dad explained. "We don't have a cat flap, for a start, so that would be a problem…"

"But we could put a litter tray in the corner of the kitchen," Jasmine suggested eagerly. "I bet the Murrays have got one, and if not, I'll buy one with my pocket money."

Mum smiled. "I thought you were saving up for my Christmas present!"

Jasmine grinned at her. "Oh, I bought your present ages ago, when you let me go Christmas shopping with Lara. Please, Mum," she added. "It's only for three weeks. I promise you won't have to do anything – I'll look after her all myself. I'll even do the vacuuming, in case Star sheds hairs on the carpet. Oh, pleeease! She'll be so miserable all on her own…"

Mum and Dad exchanged a look. "Well, I suppose we could ask Helen and Andy what they thought," Dad said, rather reluctantly.

"Yes!" Jasmine flung her arms round his neck. "This is the best Christmas present ever!"

Star sniffed thoughtfully at the pile of bags in the hallway. What was going on? Her owners seemed to be very excited, and kept running up and down the stairs.

"Oh, Star! I nearly put that on top of you. Careful, pusscat!" Helen picked her up and stroked her. "We're going to miss you. But Jasmine will look after you so well. We'd better get your things together."

Next door, Jasmine was watching the clock anxiously. "It's nearly eight o'clock. Oh, I hope they hurry. I really want to spend some time with Star before we have to go to school! There's the doorbell!" She leaped up from her chair and rushed to answer it.

Ten minutes later, the Murrays were on their way to the airport, and Jasmine was showing Star where her bowls and her litter tray were. It was so exciting watching her sniffing round the kitchen, her whiskers twitching delicately as she investigated all the interesting corners. Jasmine picked her up and stroked her lovingly, and Star rubbed her ears against Jasmine's cheek.

"Come and see my bedroom," Jasmine told her. She laughed. "You can read my cat books while I'm at school."

"Oh, I thought we'd keep her in the kitchen for now," Mum said.

"But she'd hate that, Mum! It'll be all right. Helen said she's good about using a litter tray – she won't make a mess."

Mum frowned. "Are you sure? Won't she be worried about being in a new place?"

Jasmine looked down at Star, who was purring in her arms. "She doesn't look very worried…"

Mum nodded, a little reluctantly. "I suppose not. Come on, then. We need to get to school."

Jasmine sighed. "I hope she won't be lonely without me…" she murmured.

49

Star sat in the middle of Jasmine's bed. She was rather confused. She'd been told off for being in this house before, she remembered. But she was definitely supposed to be here now, because her owners had brought her round that morning, and they'd brought her bowls and her bed too. Her bed was downstairs in the kitchen, but Jasmine's was nicer.

Star sniffed. The bed smelled like Jasmine, which was comforting. She had stayed in the kitchen for a while, but Jasmine's mum kept watching her and looking worried, and it had made Star feel worried, too. Then Jasmine's mum had gone into another room, and she hadn't liked it when Star tried to play with the wires on her computer. Helen always laughed when she did that.

Star had wondered if she'd done something wrong, if her owners didn't want her any more, but they hadn't seemed cross. They'd held her and stroked her and made a big fuss. Star was quite sure they were coming back. And meanwhile she had Jasmine, who was almost as good. Star stretched out her front paws, yawned and curled up to sleep. She hoped Jasmine would come home soon.

"Oh, Jasmine, she's gorgeous! You're so lucky!" Jasmine's friend Lara had come home from school with her to see Star. The girls had gone straight upstairs, and found the kitten snoozing on

Jasmine's bed. She was lying on her back with her paws folded on her soft cream and brown tummy, making a funny little whistling noise – a very small cat's snore.

Lara was only whispering, but Star opened one eye thoughtfully, and then bounced up, purring delightedly at Jasmine. She was back!

"Isn't she beautiful?" Jasmine said proudly. Then she sighed. "It's almost like having a cat of my own."

Lara nodded. "Three weeks is ages. Oh, I wish someone wanted me to cat-sit! I'm sure your parents will get to like her – how can they resist! You never know, then they might let you have your own cat."

Jasmine nodded, sitting down on the bed and hugging Star close. "That's what I'm really hoping, but I'm not sure it'll work. Mum was really fussing this morning, about not wanting Star to get into her office and mess up her paperwork. She wanted to keep her in the kitchen all day, but I persuaded her it wouldn't be fair. I think they only let me look after Star because they wanted to help out the people next door. Neither of them are really keen on having pets. They've said I can have a gerbil or a hamster, but I'd much, much rather have a cat."

Lara and Jasmine looked down at Star. She was purring blissfully to herself as Jasmine stroked her, in just the right itchy spot down her spine. She looked up at them, then nudged Jasmine's chin lovingly. Lara and Jasmine both sighed. Who wouldn't want such a gorgeous cat?

Over the next week, Jasmine wondered if Star had been listening to what she and Lara had said. She seemed to be doing everything she could to charm Jasmine's parents. Perhaps it was because Star felt lonely while Jasmine was at school, or perhaps it was just that she was a natural people-cat, but she put on her best manners.

On Monday afternoon, Jasmine rushed home from school and let herself in, eager to see Star. But today Star didn't come to say hello. After looking in the kitchen and her bedroom, Jasmine went to her mum's office to see if she knew where the cat was. She put her head round the office door and found Star and her mum, watching the gleams of rainbow light from the glass prism her mum had hanging in the window. Her mum was laughing as Star leaped around the room, chasing the coloured flashes on the wall.

"Aren't you supposed to be working?" she asked her mum sternly.

Mum looked guilty. "Yes. But Star came in, and she seemed to want making a fuss of. She's so funny, Jasmine – and so athletic. Look at her jumping!"

Star looked up at Jasmine lovingly, and then mewed hopefully at Jasmine's mum.

"Oh, do you want me to swing it for you again, hmm?" Mum reached up to tap the prism, sending the rainbows all round the wall again, and Star was off in a mad cat dance, leaping and patting at the pretty lights.

Jasmine huffed and went to get herself a drink. It wasn't that she didn't like her mum getting on with Star – after all, it was exactly what she'd wanted! But Jasmine did feel a tiny bit jealous. *She* played with Star. She and Lara had nipped into the pet shop on the way home, and she'd bought a jingly ball for her. But Mum's rainbow lights looked much more exciting!

Dad took a bit longer to fall for Star. He didn't really spend much time with her, and he got very ratty when he discovered she'd slept on his favourite jumper and left it covered in brown hairs. But on Sunday morning, Jasmine came downstairs and found Dad reading the newspaper, and Star sitting on the kitchen table (which she wasn't allowed to do). She was batting at the back of the paper. Every time she did it, Dad would twitch the paper straight, and Star would wait a few seconds and whack it again with her paw.

Jasmine watched her do it three more times before Dad snorted with laughter and folded up the paper. Star jumped delicately on to his lap and gazed up at him with big green eyes. Jasmine's dad looked down at her, as though he wasn't sure quite what he was supposed to do now. He put out a cautious hand and stroked her, very lightly down her back. Then he looked up at Jasmine, as if he thought she might tell him he'd done it wrong.

Jasmine sighed and shook her head, smiling. Star had managed it again. She'd even won Dad over!

Dad stroked Star again, more confidently this time. "This cat," he told Jasmine, as she fetched herself a bowl of cornflakes, "has got a real sense of humour." He reached over and grabbed a packet of cat treats that had been left on the counter. Star sat up on his lap, her tail twitching eagerly, and he fed her three, one after the other. She crunched them up quickly, with her eyes closed in delight.

"Not too many, Dad." Jasmine pointed at him with her cereal spoon. "She'll get fat. In fact..." Jasmine looked worriedly at Star's silky tummy. Was it her imagination, or was it rather larger than before? "She's getting really podgy, Dad, now that I look at her! I bet Mum's been feeding her loads of treats while I'm at school."

Jasmine didn't mention the number of times she'd saved a little bit of chicken or sausage from tea to feed to Star as an extra-special treat, but she couldn't help feeling rather guilty. She'd just wanted to make Star happy – and it was so sweet the way she nibbled the scraps off her fingers.

Jasmine's mum came downstairs and frowned when Jasmine asked her about the treats. "Well, I have given her the odd one. But not that many, Jasmine. I wouldn't have thought it would be enough to fatten her up." She eyed Star thoughtfully, as she sat on Dad's lap and washed her ears. "Hmmm. She is looking a bit fatter, you're right. Oh dear. I don't know much about cats, but

I'm sure it isn't healthy for her to be fat. She could get ill."

"I'll try and get her to do a bit more running around," Jasmine said, wondering what the Murrays would say if they came home and found they had a fat cat.

Star seemed to be able to tell that Jasmine was worried. She stopped washing and gazed lovingly at her from Dad's lap. Then she sat up on her hind legs with her front paws in the air, as though she was begging to be picked up. It was so funny Jasmine choked on her mouthful of cornflakes.

Dad grinned. "You see? She's definitely got a sense of humour!"

Chapter Four

Jasmine started Star's exercise routine the next day, when she got home from school. They had decorated the Christmas tree at the weekend, and Star had been fascinated by it. The moment Jasmine and her mum went into the kitchen for a drink, Star had climbed up it, then got stuck near the top, wailing frantically as she wobbled on her branch. Jasmine had had to rescue her, and ever since then Star had looked at the tree with great suspicion.

But Star had loved playing with the tinsel, rolling over and over and chewing it. Jasmine wasn't sure how people got cute photos of cats wearing tinsel on their collars. Star would have eaten it before anyone had a chance to get a camera out. So tinsel seemed a good idea for getting Star to jump around. It was the end of term in a couple of days. She could do lots more exercising with Star when it was the Christmas holidays. She was really looking forward to being at home and being able to play with Star all the time.

Jasmine carefully unwound a bit of silver tinsel from round the back of the tree, where no one would really notice it had gone. She crouched down in front of Star, holding the feathery silver tinsel. It shimmered and twinkled, almost as if it were alive, and Star's tail flicked back and forth as she watched it. She dabbed out a paw, and Jasmine twitched the tinsel away, so that Star missed it. The cat sprang forward, paws batting here and there, dancing and springing as Jasmine giggled and waved the tinsel for her. At one point Jasmine was sure that Star leaped at least a metre off the ground in a truly amazing jump.

Eventually Jasmine gave up as she was worn out, though Star was still full of energy. She lay on her back, tugging at the tinsel with her paws and shredding it everywhere.

"Well, that certainly ought to have worked off a few cat treats," Mum said from the doorway, where she'd been watching. "But if you do it again tomorrow, can you use string instead? We won't have any tinsel left at this rate."

Jasmine looked at the silvery bits all over the floor. "Sorry, Mum. I didn't know she'd tear it up like that. I was going to put it back on the tree."

They looked at each other, and then down at the piece of silver string that was all that was left of the tinsel.

"Maybe not..." Jasmine said, giggling, as Star abandoned the tinsel, suddenly tired out, and climbed exhaustedly into her lap. She stretched herself out over Jasmine's legs and went completely floppy, making just a very faint, wheezy purr, as though it was all she had the strength for.

Luckily, the cat dancing game worked almost as well with string, especially when Jasmine invented a brilliant new cat toy by tying some of the feathers and wool from a craft set she had on to the string to make it more exciting. They had a brilliant game with it after school on Thursday afternoon. Lara was there, too, to celebrate the start of the Christmas holidays. Mum had got them the ingredients to make some snowmen cakes, which Jasmine had seen in a magazine, and they sat in the kitchen taking turns to lick out the bowl while the cakes cooked. Lara offered a teensy bit of mixture to Star, who was sitting next to her on a chair, purring loudly.

Jasmine laughed as Star eagerly licked Lara's fingers. "Don't give her any more. She's such a piglet. Even with all the exercise she's been getting, she's still got that little round tummy. In fact it seems bigger! But I know we're not overfeeding her, I've checked the instructions on the cat food really carefully." She sighed. "I wonder if she's helping herself to food out of another cat's house? I wouldn't put it past her. She's so cute she can get away with anything."

Lara nodded. "I can't believe she won over your mum and dad, after all you said about them not liking cats."

Jasmine smiled. "It's amazing. I've loved looking after Star so much, and I'm really going to miss her when the

Murrays get back. I know she'll only be next door, but she won't be sleeping on my bed every night. I've been hoping Star might have charmed Mum and Dad enough that they'd let me have a cat of my own…"

"You really think they will?" said Lara excitedly.

Jasmine reached over and tickled Star lovingly under her chin. "I'm not sure… If the Murrays come home and say Star's got fat because we've been overfeeding her, I've got no chance!"

"But I'm sure the Murrays will see how happy Star is and how well you've looked after her. You really love her, and she adores you – you can tell she does." Lara licked her spoon.

"You wouldn't mind having a cat that wasn't Star, though?"

Jasmine looked thoughtful. "It would be weird," she admitted. "Star's so special. But I know she isn't mine. I've always known that. And you've not seen her with Helen and Andy from next door. She's clearly their cat. I mean, she likes me, but it isn't quite the same." She grinned at Lara. "I need Star number two!"

Jasmine woke up the next morning feeling so happy. At first she couldn't remember why, but then she realized it was the first proper day of the Christmas holidays, and she had a busy day of making Christmas cards and wrapping presents planned. The weather forecast had said there would be snow today, too, lots of it. It sounded as though it was going to be a real white Christmas. Jasmine smiled to herself, imagining Star chasing snowflakes, batting at them with her little paws.

She yawned and sat up, ready to stroke Star. But she wasn't there. Surprised, Jasmine looked under her duvet, in case she had crept underneath. She did that sometimes. No Star. She wasn't hiding in Jasmine's wardrobe, under the bed, or on her beanbag, either.

Jasmine threw on her dressing gown, and went downstairs, feeling worried. Star was always there when she woke up! Or sometimes she got sick of waiting and rubbed round Jasmine's face until she woke up. But she'd never gone downstairs without Jasmine before.

She found Star in the kitchen, mewing at her mum, who was scooping cat food into her bowl. She didn't even look at Jasmine, just danced and hopped round Mum's legs until she put the bowl down.

"She seems hungry this morning!" Mum commented.

"Mmm." Jasmine didn't want to say anything. She felt a bit silly, as if she was making a fuss about nothing.

But it was the same all day. Star didn't seem to want to play. She ignored the string and feathers toy when Jasmine waved it in front of her nose, and she didn't seem interested in present wrapping at all. She went and slept on the sofa for the whole afternoon, and Jasmine felt really lonely. It was stupid, because she'd only been looking after Star for a couple of weeks – but now Star didn't want to be with her it felt awful.

Jasmine watched Star anxiously as she bolted down her tea. It was the only time Star had been friendly all day – when she wanted Jasmine to feed her.

"She's starving again," Mum commented, smiling as she watched Star gobbling her food.

Jasmine nodded. "Mum, do you think Star's all right?" she asked worriedly. "She hasn't been very friendly today, not like she usually is. And she slept all afternoon!"

Mum looked at her in surprise. "Well, I don't think she's ill, not the way she's eating!"

Jasmine sighed. "I suppose not. Maybe I've been fussing over her too much."

Mum gave her a hug. "Don't worry. Maybe cats have moods just like people. Perhaps Star just feels like some time to herself today."

Star licked all the way round her food bowl, and looked at it for a moment in case it magically refilled itself. Then she turned round and walked out of the kitchen, without even looking at Jasmine.

Chapter Five

Star was feeling odd. She didn't know why, but things felt different. She knew she needed to find somewhere quiet and warm, and just curl up and be on her own for a while. But no one seemed to want her to do that!

Star loved Jasmine, and usually she adored all the attention and cuddling she got at Jasmine's house, but not right now. After breakfast that morning, she set off determined to find herself a quiet little nest.

But everywhere in the house seemed busy, and noisy, and full of people – which, considering only Jasmine and her mum were there, was rather strange. Grumpily, Star wandered back into the kitchen to see if there was any more food in her bowl. She was so hungry at the moment! Then she spotted the perfect place…

Jasmine's mum had been looking for the red tablecloth she liked to use for Christmas lunch, and she'd left a drawer in the big kitchen cupboard half open. Star peered into it interestedly. It was full of hand towels, tea towels and tablecloths. Warm, soft, clean things that would be perfect to snuggle up and snooze on. Star wondered why she had never noticed it before – it was just right! She stepped in and curled up at the back of the drawer, yawning and closing her eyes.

Some time later, Star woke up to find herself in complete darkness. She opened her eyes very wide, her heart thudding, unable to think where she was. Then she remembered. Her soft, cosy nest. What had happened to it? Why had it gone dark? She edged forward to where the opening had been and pawed at the wooden walls. She was shut in a tight, dark box! Panicking, Star scratched and scuffled at the front of the drawer, and mewed frantically.

Jasmine and her mum were making

cards at the kitchen table. "That sounds like Star," said Jasmine. "I was wondering where she was. She's shut in somewhere, Mum!"

"I don't understand," Jasmine's mum muttered, opening cupboards. "Where can she be? Oh! Oh dear, the drawer!"

Star blinked and cowered as her nest moved sharply, bumping her head against the top of the drawer. She was pulled out into the light, huddling against the towels.

"Oh, poor Star…" Jasmine lifted her out, and Star snuggled gratefully against her.

"What on earth was she doing in there?" Jasmine's mum asked, sounding rather guilty – she had been the one who shut Star in.

"I suppose she was just looking for somewhere cosy to sleep," Jasmine suggested. "It wasn't your fault, Mum, you couldn't have known she was there." She stroked Star's head gently. "I know we're cutting back, but I think she really deserves a cat treat!"

Mum and Jasmine went back to card-making, and Star played half-heartedly with some pencils, but she couldn't enjoy the game properly. She was still feeling the need to find herself a quiet place to rest, and she sneaked away to go searching again. This time she found a space under the stairs. It was quiet and dark, and it didn't have a door that anyone could close on her by accident. There were lots of odd things stored under there: wellies, roller skates, and a big basket full of gloves and scarves and hats. Star scrambled up the side and turned round several times, purring throatily. This was just right. She would stay here.

But it didn't last. Star was sleeping peacefully when she felt her hiding place shudder as Jasmine raced up the stairs over her head, calling for her. And then Jasmine's mum hauled out the vacuum cleaner, which was right next to her basket bed.

"Oh, Star, I didn't see you. She's down here, Jasmine!" Mum called. And Jasmine came dashing down the stairs again, thud, thump, thud, and picked Star up for a cuddle.

Star was still half-asleep, and she was grumpy. She didn't *want* to be picked up. She wanted to be left alone. Crossly, she gave a loud hiss, lashed out with her claws and scratched Jasmine's arm.

Jasmine was so surprised she yelled and dropped Star, who hissed and shot into the kitchen. There she yowled at Jasmine's mum until she opened the back door.

Jasmine clutched her arm, which was oozing a few spots of blood. She entered the kitchen just in time to see Star's grey and brown striped tail disappearing round the back door. Then she sat down at the kitchen table and cried. Star had scratched her – and then Jasmine had scared her so much by shouting that she'd run away!

Star stayed out in the garden until it got dark, hiding under a clump of bushes.

She was shivering from the cold and knew she couldn't stay out all night. But she'd spent a long time trying to work out where she could go and hadn't found anywhere good. Everywhere was too busy, too full of people.

She crept out from under her bush and sneaked over to the hole under the fence. She didn't quite have the energy to climb over the fence right now. She dug a little with her claws, widening the hole, then squeezed herself underneath. She had been back to her own garden quite a lot while she was staying at Jasmine's house, trying to make sure all the local cats still knew it was hers. Perhaps she could go and make a nest in the bramble patch? She shivered again. No, it was far too cold, colder than she'd ever felt it, and the ground was frozen hard. She needed somewhere really warm.

Her house! Of course. She had been back a few times since she'd been staying with Jasmine, to see if the Murrays had come back, but it felt strange and empty. Now the quiet house felt like just what she needed.

Eagerly, Star scurried over to the door and nosed at her cat flap, squeezing herself in.

It was so quiet. No one around. Quite warm, or at least warmer than the bramble bushes. Perfect. She looked round the kitchen thoughtfully, trying to think of a good place to go.

After her experience with drawers at Jasmine's house, she didn't want anywhere too small and tight. Star set off upstairs, and tried all the beds, but they weren't right either – too out in the open. At last, in the smaller bedroom, she found the airing cupboard. The door was shut, but it only had a light catch, and the door itself was made of wooden slats that were perfect for claws to hook between.

Star pulled it open and crept in, sniffing delightedly at the clean, fresh smell. The floor was covered in a pile of old towels, and she curled up on them, closing her eyes peacefully. She was home. Just in time.

Chapter Six

It was almost bedtime. By now Jasmine was panicking. She couldn't find Star anywhere. She'd even checked the kitchen cupboard drawer, just in case.

"She's run away because I shouted at her!" Jasmine wailed. "It's all my fault!"

"She's probably just out exploring," Jasmine's mum suggested, trying to calm her down. "You know she likes to go off and sniff around in those brambles next door."

Jasmine bolted out into the dark garden, without even putting on her coat, and raced down to the end. She climbed up her mum's rockery – which she definitely wasn't allowed to do – and peered over at the brambly bit at the end of the Murrays' garden. A few tiny snowflakes drifted gently past her nose, and she shivered.

"Star! Star! Here, puss, puss…" She tried again and again, but no little stripy cat appeared out of the trailing branches, looking up at her lovingly.

Jasmine wandered sadly back up the garden. She looked so unhappy that her mum didn't bother telling her off.

"She isn't there."

"You don't know that, Jasmine. She might just not want to come out."

"But why?" Jasmine cried. "Why doesn't she want to play any more? What have I done to make her not like me? I was supposed to be looking after her! She used to like me, I know she did, but she even scratched me! She's never done that before."

She slumped down in a kitchen chair, and her mum sat down next to her. "Jasmine, it isn't your fault. You've looked after her really well. Cats are like that sometimes. They can get touchy and grumpy, just like people can. She's probably stalking blackbirds in a garden a few doors down. I'm sure she'll be back soon."

Jasmine gave her a disbelieving look. "It's starting to snow out there, Mum! It's freezing! Star wouldn't want to stay out in this weather – she likes being warm." Jasmine looked over at Star's bowl, which was full of food. "She hasn't even come back for her tea and she must be really hungry by now. Oh, what if she doesn't come back? What are we going to do? How will we tell Andy and Helen?"

Mum thought for a moment, then smiled. "Do you know what I think, Star's probably gone back home!"

Jasmine's mouth opened, then she grinned back at her mum. "Of course she has!" She hugged her round the waist lovingly. "Oh, Mum, you're so clever, why didn't I think of that?"

The house felt strange, rather cold and very quiet. Jasmine couldn't help feeling guilty, as though she was trespassing. She was glad Mum had come with her.

She had hoped that Star would come out to meet her as soon as she opened the door, but no little stripy cat appeared, mewing in welcome. Then Jasmine had an awful thought – what if Star had accidentally got herself shut in somewhere like she had earlier? That was only because Mum had shut the drawer, of course, but Star could easily have got herself trapped if a door had swung closed. And no one had been here to let her out! Jasmine ran through the house, calling and calling for Star, until her voice hurt and Mum told her gently to stop.

Tucked away inside the warm airing cupboard, Star could hear Jasmine calling her name. She was tempted to mew and let Jasmine know where she was — she missed her soft stroking, the loving whispers, and the delicious treats Jasmine always had for her. But for now she needed to be alone. She wasn't ready quite yet. Soon.

Mum had her arm round Jasmine as they walked back home. "She'll turn up," she told her, trying to sound encouraging. "You know Helen said she'd been wandering a bit."

"Did you find her?" Dad opened the front door as they came down the path.

Jasmine shook her head sadly, and Dad gave her a hug. "I'll help you look for her tomorrow," he promised. But he gave his wife a worried frown over Jasmine's head.

"I don't think we'll ever find her!" Jasmine wailed.

"Oh, darling, you're getting way ahead of yourself! If she isn't back in the morning, then we'll go and look for her. But she will be. You'll see."

Just before Jasmine went to bed that night, she went to draw her bedroom curtains and peered out at the night-filled garden. There were deep shadows everywhere and it looked frightening. Jasmine hated to think of Star out there somewhere all on her own. Last time Star had been out at night,

Jasmine had rescued her. But now she wasn't even sure Star would want to be rescued. Or at least not by her.

"If only I hadn't shouted at her like that," she whispered miserably to her reflection in the window.

Suddenly the dark sky filled with thick snowflakes, and Jasmine watched sadly as they began to cover the garden in frozen whiteness.

Chapter Seven

To: Jasmine
From: Helen Murray
Subject: Hello!

We're having a wonderful time. Saw a newspaper
and can't believe it's snowing back at home,
and we're sunbathing and swimming in the sea
here! Hope you're really enjoying it though
— it's the first time Star has seen snow.
Make a snowman for us!
Love from Helen and Andy

PS Happy Christmas! Go next door and look
in the cupboard under the sink, just a
little present for you and one for Star, her
favourite salmon treats!

A fat tear splashed on to the keyboard. It was snowing still, just in time for a white Christmas, the first one for years. Everyone was really excited about it, but Jasmine couldn't care less. Lara had invited her to go and build an igloo in her garden, but Jasmine couldn't face it. She just kept imagining poor Star, shivering in the middle of a snowstorm, ice dripping off her whiskers. It was the worst Christmas ever. She couldn't even feel excited about presents.

"Do you think we should call and tell them she's gone?" Jasmine asked her mum sadly. The Murrays' email said they'd got her a present, to say thank you for looking after Star so well... She felt so miserably guilty.

"They left the number of their hotel, didn't they?"

"Yes, they did," said Mum. "But Star's only been gone one night, and we don't want to ruin their holiday. There's nothing they could do. I'm sure she'll be back by the time they fly home in a few days anyway."

Jasmine nodded. She supposed Mum was right. It would only make the Murrays really sad, and there was a chance she might still find her...

She'd spent the morning going up and down the street with Dad, peering under bushes and looking behind walls. Jasmine had even asked everyone she knew in the street to look in their sheds and garages, and tell their neighbours. Feeling helpless, she went to put on her coat. She didn't really think she'd find Star now, but she couldn't give up. It was Christmas Eve tomorrow. How could she leave Star lost out in the snow at Christmas?

"Are you going out again?" her mum asked worriedly. "Honestly, Jasmine, you'll freeze! Do you want me to come?"

Jasmine shook her head. "It's OK. Maybe later."

She was plodding up the pavement through the snow, which was already turning grey and slushy, when she had a thought. The Murrays' email had said they'd left some of Star's favourite salmon cat treats, and Jasmine knew she really did love those ones. She turned into the most adoring little cat ever when you were about to open a packet, weaving round your legs, mewing loudly. Perhaps if Star was hiding out in one of the gardens somewhere – and that was what Jasmine was hoping – she'd come back if she smelled those yummy salmon treats?

Jasmine dashed back home to fetch the Murrays' keys and scuttled down next door's path.

Of course she shouldn't be opening Star's present before Christmas, Jasmine thought to herself as she ripped open the shiny paper, but this was an emergency.

She was just tearing at the foil pouch with her nails when she heard it. A loud piercing, demanding, very squeaky mew. From upstairs.

Star was here!

Although that didn't sound quite like Star. Could another cat have got in?

Jasmine crept up the stairs, feeling half-hopeful, half-scared. She wasn't quite sure what to expect – even if it was Star up there, would she be happy to see her? She'd been so grumpy the day she disappeared.

The strange mewing continued as Jasmine reached the landing. She opened one of the bedroom doors and peered round. It seemed empty. But then the squeaky mew came again, and she realized that there was another door, over in the corner, almost hidden by the wardrobe. And it was very slightly open.

"Star?" Jasmine whispered nervously.

There was a moment's silence, and then Jasmine heard a very familiar purr. Star! It was definitely her, and she was purring in welcome. Jasmine wanted to race across the room and hug her, but she told herself to be calm and not get too excited. It was probably her being too enthusiastic that had made Star leave in the first place. She walked quietly over to the airing cupboard and very gently opened the door.

There was Star, lying curled on a pile of towels and purring delightedly at Jasmine.

And snuggled up next to her were two tiny newborn kittens.

Chapter Eight

Star stared up at Jasmine, purring proudly. She was very pleased that Jasmine had found her – she wanted to show off her beautiful babies. And she was absolutely starving – she hadn't eaten for a whole day now, and she'd been feeding her kittens, too. She had thought about going to find Jasmine, and some food, but she hadn't wanted to leave her kittens – she knew they needed her. She had hoped and hoped that Jasmine would come, and now she had. She miaowed at Jasmine, who seemed to be holding a food packet.

Jasmine crouched down and poured some salmon treats out into her hand. "Oh, you must be starved, poor Star," she murmured, gently scattering them in front of Star's nose, without getting too close to the kittens. She didn't want to upset Star. Luckily, Star didn't seem to mind being found, but Jasmine knew she would be very protective of her little ones. She sat back on her heels, a little way away from the cupboard, and laughed to herself. "I thought I'd been feeding you too much, Star! I thought you were just getting podgy, but you were going to have kittens!"

Star licked her kittens' heads fondly with her own little pink tongue. Jasmine's eyes filled with tears. It was so grown up, such a mother cat thing to do, and Star was only a baby herself, really too young to have kittens.

"But I guess you didn't know you were too young," Jasmine murmured. "Wow. Andy and Helen have got three cats now; they're so lucky!" She looked admiringly at the kittens. They were about as long as two of her fingers. One of them was a gorgeous stripy ginger, and the other looked like a tiny baby Star – only with slightly more grey in her tabby fur. Their eyes were closed, and their ears were almost invisible, still tucked against their heads.

Star gave her a slightly anxious look, and Jasmine smiled. "They're beautiful. Beautiful kittens." She couldn't tell if they were boys or girls. Then she frowned slightly. She hoped Star was OK. Was there anything she ought to do for her? Did she need to go to a vet?

Jasmine carefully backed away from the cupboard, not wanting to startle Star or the kittens – although they were fast asleep and didn't look like much could disturb them right now. "I'll be back soon," she murmured. "And I'll bring you some more food and water, and – and a litter tray."

Jasmine raced downstairs and back to her own house. "Mum! Mum!" she called excitedly.

Her mum rushed out of the kitchen. "Have you found her? Oh, you have, haven't you? Well done, Jasmine!" She peered over Jasmine's shoulder, expecting to see Star following her. "But where is she?"

Jasmine beamed, and hugged her. She'd almost forgotten how miserable and frightened she had been about losing Star, and now an incredible relief flooded over her in waves. She needed to hold on to someone. "You're not going to believe it," she said into her mum's shoulder.

"What? Has she been somewhere really obvious all the time? What's happened?"

"She's in next door's airing cupboard." Jasmine grinned at her. "And she's had kittens!"

"No!" Jasmine's mum gasped. "You mean it? Star has? How could we not have noticed she was pregnant?"

Jasmine laughed. "I don't know! I guess we just thought she was too young. There are only two kittens, so I suppose that's why she wasn't really that big. We did think she was fat, didn't we? I need to go and find all my cat books, Mum, I need to know what we should do!"

Jasmine was very careful not to upset Star by fussing over her and the kittens too much. She knew now that Star had been grumpy because she was about to have the kittens, and her cat instincts were telling her she needed to hide away somewhere safe. But she was pretty sure that Star would still be touchy about anyone going too close. So she left kitten food – her books said that was what Star needed right now, as it was high in energy – and water bowls and a litter tray just outside the cupboard. She then strictly rationed herself to a five-minute visit every couple of hours. Her mum had rung the vet whose number the Murrays had left. The receptionist had said that it sounded like Star was doing brilliantly all by herself, but to ring if there were any problems and the vet would come out and see her.

It had gone from being the worst Christmas Jasmine could have imagined to the absolute best. She spent the time between her visits to Star and the kittens looking up kitten-care on the computer and nibbling her nails, wishing the time would go faster.

"I do wish we could stroke the kittens," she said to her mum the next morning. "I know we shouldn't, because they're too little, but they look so soft and cuddly."

"Mmm." Jasmine's mum wasn't listening properly, as she was trying to work out exactly how long she had to cook the Christmas turkey for the next day. "Do you think we should have parsnips, Jasmine? I can't remember if you like them."

"I don't," Jasmine said. "Ooh, Mum, we'll have to take Star some Christmas dinner tomorrow. Just a little bit. Please?"

Mum shook her head, laughing. "Poor Helen and Andy, coming home to find a cat eating Christmas dinner in their airing cupboard!"

Jasmine smiled. "They won't mind,"

she said. She knew how much the Murrays adored Star. "They'll be so excited about the kittens. It's going to be such a brilliant surprise. They're so lucky, coming back to three cats instead of one!"

Mum looked thoughtful. "I don't know. Three cats is quite a lot, all at once. But I'm sure they'll be able to find good homes for the kittens."

Jasmine blinked back sudden tears. She hadn't thought that the Murrays might not keep the kittens – she'd been really looking forward to having three cats next door now! She didn't notice that Mum was watching her, a strange, thoughtful expression on her face.

"I'll just go and check on them all," Jasmine muttered. "I'll take Star some more of that special cat milk." Mum had made an emergency rush to the pet shop yesterday to buy some kitten food and some milk that was made to be safe for cats' stomachs.

She sat by the airing cupboard door watching Star, who was looking down at her feeding babies with a very contented look on her face.

"Oh, Star, I hope the Murrays will keep them," Jasmine murmured. "I don't want you to lose your kittens!"

But Star wasn't listening. She was gently licking the ginger kitten's ears, as if making sure they were perfectly clean was the most important thing in the world.

Jasmine woke up very early on Christmas morning. She smiled delightedly as she felt the heavy weight of her stocking next to her feet and sat up to see if she could feel what was in it.

Then she frowned. Was that mewing? Jasmine put on her bedside light and listened again. Star was safe next door, and she'd checked on her last thing the night before, but – yes, there it was again. Jasmine ran downstairs and unlocked the back door to find Star standing there, with the little tabby kitten held in her mouth. Star dashed inside – probably she was worried about the kitten catching cold, Jasmine thought, looking out at the garden as she closed the door. There had been another snowfall in the night, and the grass was covered in a fresh white layer, which looked weird and blue-grey in the darkness.

"Where are you going, Star?" she asked, following the little cat as she trotted through the dark hallway. She flinched as Star started to climb the stairs, determinedly heaving the kitten up each step. Jasmine desperately wanted to help, but wasn't sure if Star would let her.

Eventually, they reached the landing, and Star made for Jasmine's bedroom, where she stared meaningfully at the wardrobe.

"Oh!" Jasmine laughed. "You want to have your bed in my wardrobe?" she asked delightedly. She opened the door at once and quickly pulled out her trainers, then fluffed an old fleece blanket into a comfy nest for Star and the kittens.

Star scrambled in and dropped the kitten gently on the blanket, where it wriggled and made a faint, squeaky little mew. Then Star trotted off to go and fetch the other kitten.

By lunchtime, Star was well settled, with her food bowls next to the wardrobe. Mum had brought her little extra morsels of turkey, and Jasmine had even hung some tinsel over the wardrobe door, to make it look Christmassy.

Jasmine had wondered if she might have to go and sleep on the sofa, but Star didn't seem to mind her being there – and so Jasmine was able to watch her and the kittens a lot more. They were so cute. She was sure that the little tabby one was going to open its eyes soon. They were both gorgeous, of course, but the tabby baby was so like Star, Jasmine couldn't help loving it most of all. She was almost sure it was a girl kitten, it looked so like its mum.

It was rather a strange Christmas Day, but peeping in at the sleeping kittens, Jasmine thought it was the loveliest she'd ever had.

Two days later, the Murrays arrived home. They hurried next door to Jasmine's house as soon as they'd dropped off their bags.

Jasmine answered the door, hugging her secret to herself and trying not to giggle.

"Come and see!" she told them.

"Is Star asleep on your bed?" Helen asked, as they followed Jasmine upstairs.

"Not quite," Jasmine said mysteriously. She led them into her room, and stood back so they could see the scene in her wardrobe.

Star seemed to know she had visitors. She was posed like a queen, and Jasmine was sure she was eyeing the kittens anxiously to make sure they were looking gorgeous, too.

"Goodness!" Helen crouched down to look. "I had no idea she was pregnant!"

"Nor did we," Jasmine explained. "She started behaving a bit strangely, and then she disappeared, and... We did wonder if it was because she was really missing you. But actually she was having babies in your airing cupboard! Mum cleaned it up," she added.

"Clever little Star..." Helen murmured, and Andy shook his head in amazement. "Talk about keeping it quiet. So now we've got three cats!"

"You're so lucky," Jasmine sighed, and Helen looked at her thoughtfully. Leaving Jasmine to tell Andy the whole story right from the beginning, she beckoned Jasmine's mum out of the room.

They came back a couple of minutes later, just as Jasmine was describing

Star arriving at the back door on Christmas morning.

"Your mum's agreed we'd better let them all stay here for the moment. Star probably won't want to be moved," Helen said. "As long as you don't mind sharing your bedroom, that is?"

"Of course not!" said Jasmine. "What will you do when the kittens are bigger?" she asked. "Will you keep them all?" She wasn't sure that she wanted to know the answer.

"Well, three cats is rather a lot…" Helen said, smiling at Jasmine's mum. "I really love the little ginger one – I've a feeling he takes after Tiger, that handsome ginger cat down the road."

Jasmine gulped. They didn't want the tabby kitten! She couldn't bear the idea of her special little Christmas kitten being unwanted. It was so unfair.

She almost didn't hear Helen as she went on, "But I've had an idea. One way that she could have her own home and stay close to her mum."

Jasmine looked up, her eyes full of hope. "You mean…"

Helen grinned at her. "Why not?"

Jasmine looked over at her parents. There was no way Mum and Dad would let her. Was there?

Mum smiled. "Would you like to keep her, Jasmine? You know your dad and I have never been keen on having a cat, but Star won me over. She's so sweet. Your dad really took to having a cat as well – he was so upset when Star was missing. I'd been wondering whether we could keep one of the kittens even before Helen asked me," Mum went on. "You looked after Star so well. Dad and I were really proud of you."

"And as the kitten practically started her life in your wardrobe, I don't really think we could say no!" Dad laughed.

Jasmine looked down at the little silvery kitten with new eyes. She could be hers! Star gazed at her lovingly, as though she approved of the idea, too.

"What will you call her, Jasmine?" Mum asked.

Jasmine thought for a moment. Something Christmassy. Then she smiled, remembering Star's mum's favourite game. "Tinsel," she said, reaching out, very gently, to stroke her new cat.

HOLLY WEBB

Holly Webb started out as a children's
book editor and wrote her first series for
the publisher she worked for. She has been
writing ever since, with over one hundred
books to her name. Holly lives in Berkshire,
with her husband and three children.
Holly's pet cats are always nosying around
when she is trying to type on her laptop.

For more information
about Holly Webb visit:

www.holly-webb.com